BAG MAN

MICHAEL KINGSWOOD

 Created with Vellum

Contents

About This Book

A mysterious bag that everyone wants. An employer who is as dangerous as she is beautiful. A man on the run.

It was supposed to be a routine pickup, just another day on the job.

If only it had been that easy.

Bag Man is a 5,600 word short mystery.

Enjoy the book! After you're done, please come to Michael's website and sign up for his mailing list at michaelkingswood.com/newsletter-signup/. Guaranteed to be spam free, he uses it to announce new releases and special promotions for his fans.

Bag Man

Pain flared from the wound in Jayme's abdomen, pulsing in time with the lifeblood spurting from the cut. He gritted his teeth to keep from crying out, but a guttural groan still issued from his lips. Though he knew it was futile, he nevertheless pressed his hands against the wound, trying in vain to stem the flow of blood and to preserve his life.

"I can't believe that bitch pulled a knife on me."

In spite of himself, Jayme laughed at his partner's remark, though doing so caused the pain to intensify, turning his guffaw into another groan that was almost, but not quite, a scream.

Beside him on the floor, Rolf also lay wounded, though he was not nearly in as bad a state. His left arm hung limply, his shoulder dislocated at least, and he had a deep cut in his right thigh. But, unlike Jayme, he would clearly live through the day unless something drastic happened.

The bastard.

Of course, it looked like something drastic was about to happen. Jayme turned his head to see Ismerelda stepping through the front door, along with her two guards. Had he been healthy, Jayme would have disregarded the guards out of hand; they were brainless thugs who knew only brute force, not subtlety. But in his current state…

With a rueful smile, Jayme drew in a breath and spoke. Or rather, he tried to, but all that came out was a rattling grunt, itself almost a groan. He swallowed, the act itself all but useless considering his mouth was dry as a desert. But it worked, for when he tried to speak again, words actually came forth.

"She…cut your leg," he said. "You *shot* me."

Rolf actually looked embarrassed. "Yeah, well," he said, "sorry 'bout that. Wasn't my fault. Just business, right?"

Right. Just business.

THE DAY STARTED out promisingly enough.

Jayme and Rolf were on assignment. They met at 10:30 and drove to their meet in the back room at Fabricio's, a small coffee shop in a strip mall not far from the airport that was owned by a guy who was friendly with Jayme's employers. For a little kickback each month, he looked the other way at some of the business deals that went down there. It was a convenient setup, especially since Fabricio made some of the best crepes in town, and great coffee to go with them.

They were supposed to meet up with a man from Puerto Rico about a bag. They were to know him by the black fedora he liked to wear. Simple enough; they had done similar jobs countless times. Except when they showed up at the meet, there was no man present who met that description.

There was, however, an extremely attractive woman in a tight-fitting blue dress. Tall - maybe five foot ten, without her high heels - and with a body that any red-blooded man would die for, it was easy to miss looking at her face. Which would be a mistake because she had the deepest blue eyes Jayme had ever seen, lips of deep red, and a heart-shaped face that would stand out in any beauty pageant, all framed by hair so blond it was almost white.

He should have known it was a set-up.

They waited for fifteen minutes, and spent most of the time staring at the woman as they sipped a couple cups of coffee. She sat at a table in the corner by herself, sipping a cup of tea, reading the paper, and pretending not to notice their stares. Finally, Jayme decided the meet was blown and nudged Rolf, who nodded reluctantly and stood along with Jayme. They only made a single step toward the door before the thugs stepped inside.

They were not particularly tall, but broad and muscular, with similar enough bodies and faces that Jayme assumed they were brothers. They wore suits that were neither cheap nor expensive and simple black sunglasses. Their suit coats bulged ever so slightly on their left sides beneath their armpits. An untrained eye would not even notice it, but Jayme was not untrained. They were packing heat and, from the look of them, they probably would not hesitate for long in using it.

"Why don't you gentlemen sit down," a sultry voice spoke from behind them.

Jayme and Rolf exchanged glances. Rolf shrugged and turned around, and Jayme followed him over to the woman's table.

She had set the paper down and was staring at them with a little smile on her lips, the kind of smile that said she knew secrets they would kill to learn. As they approached, the woman picked up her tea cup again and gestured with her free hand toward the chairs across from herself as she took another sip.

There was nothing to do but sit down and see where this was going, so Jayme hesitated only a heartbeat before unbuttoning his sports coat and taking one of the two chairs. Rolf settled in as well, looking more casual in his jeans and leather jacket - Jayme had never been able to get him to dress the part better - and the waiting game began.

In tense situations like the one Jayme found himself in that morning, some people seemed to find it amusing to wait, as though a few moments of silence would make him squirm. He supposed maybe your everyday Joe on the street would find that silence uncomfortable, especially with a couple of armed thugs at his back. But Jayme had long since learned that there can be great advantage in speaking second and besides, he hated playing stupid games. So he sat still and stared at the woman for a long few moments, drinking in the sight of her while he waited. It was far from the most unpleasant staredown he had ever participated in.

The woman's smile broadened slightly and she sniffed, then set her teacup down. "I'm afraid your contact won't be making an appearance this morning," she said in the same sultry voice that she used to 'invite' them over.

"Not sure what you're talking about, miss," Rolf replied with aplomb. "We're just here for coffee."

She sniffed dismissively and shot Rolf an annoyed look. "Please," she said, her tone scornful. "I think we can skip the games and get right to the point, don't you?"

Jayme and Rolf traded another glance. Rolf

looked almost apologetic as he shrugged slightly in the manner that said he would let Jayme take the lead.

"Fair enough," Jayme said. "I assume you know where he is, miss…" He let the sentence trail away into a question.

"You may call me Ismerelda. And yes, I do."

Jayme leaned back in his chair and sighed. "And I suppose you're not going to tell us." He hated when this sort of thing happened.

Ismerelda surprised him, though. Her smile grew and she shook her head. "Oh I am absolutely going to tell you." She traced one finger along the rim of her teacup, making a soft humming sound despite it not being made of crystal. "But I want something in return."

This was getting tiresome. "Look lady," Jayme said, "I don't have time for this." Pressing his palms against the tabletop, Jayme moved to stand up. The sound of two hammers being pulled back behind him made him stop.

Ismerelda tsk'd softly. "Mr. Hawthorn, I think you and Mr. Steinman really want to hear what I have to say."

That got Jayme's attention, and he slowly lowered himself back into his chair. How had she known his name? From the corner of his eye, Jayme saw that Rolf was thinking similarly, and that her knowledge took him off guard. Shoving sudden doubt away, Jayme put his poker face on and twirled his index finger in the air in a 'get on with it' motion.

Ismerelda's eyebrows quirked upward slightly as Jayme's gesture, but if it irked her she did not let it show in her tone of voice. "I want the bag."

Jayme was so stunned he laughed before he could stop himself. The utter gall of this broad!

He got himself under control after a few seconds, but he could see his laughter had annoyed her in a way his gesture had not. The smile vanished from her face, replaced by a tight little scowl, and her brow furrowed as she narrowed her eyes at him.

"That was not a joke, Mr. Hawthorn."

Jayme snorted and leaned forward. "It sounded like one to me. That bag belongs to someone else, and it's my job to get it to him. I don't know who you think you are, but if you think I'm just going to renege on a contract because you say so, you've got another thing coming."

Ismerelda surprised him again. "It does belong to someone, Mr. Hawthorn. Me."

"You?"

She nodded. "The courier you were to meet stole it from my business associate. It's contents are quite valuable to me, and I want them back."

That did not make any sense. "Why don't you just take it back then? If you know where he is…"

"The situation is…complicated. If I take a direct hand in this, it may upset some very carefully laid plans, and I don't want that to happen."

"So just send other goons. We have people we work for, too, and they spent good money for that bag. They won't appreciate it if we just blow them off to help you."

Ismerelda smiled again, that teasing smile that made him question his assumptions. Slowly, ever so slowly, she lifted a small handbag, barely more than a pouch really, up onto the table from the seat next to her. The bag was held shut by a small clasp at its top, which she flipped open with a casual flick of her fingers.

"I don't think they will mind."

As she spoke, she withdrew a small stack of

photographs, old-school polaroids from the look of them, and tossed them onto the table.

Jayme glanced down at the photos and had to stop himself from gasping in shocked surprise. Rolf failed to do the same. Each photograph showed a dead man, shot through the temple with a small caliber bullet. Jayme recognized all of them.

"As you can see," Ismerelda went on, "your employers no longer care about my bag." Resting her elbows on the table, she folded her hands together and rested her chin upon them. She would have been cute enough to kiss right then, except for her demonstrated ruthlessness. How the hell...

"How the hell did *you* get to *them*?" Rolf said, echoing Jayme's thoughts.

Ismerelda smirked. "A girl needs her secrets, Mr. Steinman." Her gaze flittered between them for a moment before settling back onto Jayme. "Since you are independent contractors now, it would be in your interest to help me. It is better than the alternative." Her eyes flicked down toward the photos again.

No mistaking that threat. Crap.

"What's our cut?"

"Ten grand. Each. And I'll make a point of mentioning how professional you are to my friends, should they need assistance later." Her smile was almost mocking now.

"Riiiight." Jayme looked at Rolf.

The other man wore a deep frown, but when he met Jayme's gaze, he shrugged. The shrug spoke volumes.

Jayme had to admit, he had a point. What were they supposed to do, get killed from loyalty to their old bosses? He snorted inwardly; he had not liked them, and certainly only respected the paychecks they handed out. As far as Jayme was concerned, they got what they deserved.

So what the hell, a bird in the hand, and all that.

"Ok, you've got a deal."

"Excellent."

In retrospect, it was not his smartest move ever.

SINCE THEIR ORIGINAL contact was coming from Puerto Rico, most people who wanted to track him down would have looked for him in hotels close to the airport. He picked one far away.

Smart. Professionally smart.

The Indigo Motel sat on a frontage road that ran alongside the Interstate, about twenty miles from the airport. It was old, probably built in the 50s, and was badly in need of a paint job and remodeling. It was the sort of place that probably was not very particular about its clientele.

Jayme drove his Mustang past the motel and scoped out the area. There were five other cars visible, all non-descript late-model sedans of various makes. None would particularly stand out, and any could be their man's vehicle.

"Room twenty-five, right there." Rolf pointed at the door in question as they rolled past and narrowed his eyes, studying it intently. "Curtains are drawn. Can't tell if he's in there."

The parking spot in front of the room was empty, but that did not mean anything. A pro would park elsewhere, maybe, to throw off the scent.

"Let's circle back in a few minutes," Jayme said, and got a nod of agreement from Rolf.

They stopped for a short while at a gas station

a couple miles away to top off the tank and use the facilities. Then they reversed course.

A new car was parked in the Motel lot, a yellow Mazda coup that stood out like a sore thumb among all the other vehicles there. As they drove past, Jayme saw a woman step out of the driver's side door and take a look around.

She was average height, dressed simply in jeans and a loose t-shirt, and sunglasses. She had strawberry blonde hair that was pulled back from her eyes and tied in a small bun on the back of her head, like a military woman who does not want a short haircut will do. Jayme would not have looked at her twice, except she went up to Room Twenty-Five and knocked on the door.

"Well, well," Jayme said as they left the motel behind. "Our man's got company."

"Didn't look like a hooker."

Jayme snorted. "It's a little early in the day for that."

Rolf chuckled. "Not really. You can find a working girl twenty-four hours a day, if you know where to look."

Jayme rolled his eyes. Rolf was sometimes a bit crass. "Whatever."

They parked in a lot a few hundred yards away from the motel and settled in to wait. There were still several hours of daylight remaining, and it would be better to do the job while the guy was alone, anyway.

Turns out, they did not have to wait long.

Maybe ten minutes later, the door to room twenty-five opened and the woman stepped back out into the sunlight.

"That was quick," Rolf said, and smirked.

Always in the gutter, he was. Jayme rolled his

eyes again, then returned his attention to their quarry.

The woman got into her car, but did not drive off immediately. What was she waiting for?

Then a man emerged from the room. He was thin, a bit taller than average, and wore a dark business suit. He paused for a moment just outside his door to don a fedora, then walked over to the woman's car and got into the passenger seat, pausing only to shove the bulky duffle bag he carried into the back seat.

Jayme leaned forward, his eyes narrowing. The duffle bag.

"Looks like he had another meet set up besides ours," Rolf said.

Jayme nodded slowly. It almost made sense; the man probably would have wanted to shop the bag around, get the best price. But the meet was all set up. He would not want to piss off the kinds of people Jayme and Rolf worked for, not over a few bucks. Unless...

"Motherfucker," he said, sudden anger making him grip the steering wheel tightly enough that his knuckles turned white.

Rolf glanced at him questioningly. He did not see it.

"That fucker knew Ismerelda was after him, so he set up the meet with us as a diversion. He's been playing us from the start."

Rolf's sudden scowl likely matched Jayme's own. "Let's get him."

The Mazda pulled out of the Motel parking lot and turned left. It passed Jayme and Rolf's position, and Jayme got a good look in the windows for a moment. The woman was laughing about something.

Jayme started his Mustang back up and put it in gear. Time to do the job.

THE MAZDA GOT onto the Interstate and drove west for forty-five minutes, well past the outskirts of suburbia and into the boonies, then turned off onto a two-lane country road. Jayme followed at a discreet distance, being careful to keep one or two cars between himself and the Mazda; he did not want to spook the game too early.

The country road twisted and turned through sprawling woods and around several small hills, and Jayme lost sight of the other car on more than one occasion. But always it was there again when he rounded the bend.

Until suddenly it was not.

He checked the rearview mirror.

Nothing.

He looked to either side.

Nothing. What the hell?

"Maybe they sped up." From the tone of his voice, Rolf did not believe that any more than Jayme did. The pair in the Mazda had given them the slip. But where?

A half-mile up the road was a small turnoff. Jayme used it to make a three-point turn, then drove back the way he came, more slowly than before.

He saw it this time. Halfway through the turn, a small dirt trail, mostly hidden from view by large bushes until he was right on it, led away from the road to the right.

Jayme stopped the Mustang and looked down the trail. It curved to the left about a hundred yards down; the trees obscured everything beyond that. But there were fresh tire marks.

They had to have come this way; there was nowhere else for them to go.

He and Rolf exchanged looks. Rolf, looking grim, reached beneath his leather jacket and un-snapped the tab holding his Beretta into its shoulder holster.

Jayme's Sig was nestled into a holster at the small of his back; it would be hard to draw in a hurry while he was sitting down. He took a moment to pull it out and check he had remembered to chamber a round earlier. Then he tucked it into the space between his seat and the center console and turned off onto the dirt trail.

He drove slowly, but it made no difference. The Mustang was not designed for smooth travel off of pavement. It jounced all over the place, bumping and swaying. Before they reached the bend to the left, Rolf was already holding onto the hand grip on the door and looking a bit green; he got motion sickness from the strangest things.

Not that Jayme liked the ride any more than he did. The constant bumping began to do a number on his back; it ached some days, and the bumping did not help matters.

They rounded the bend, then a second that turned to the right. The trees began to thin ahead as the trail approached yet another turn to the left. Jayme could just make out a small two-story cabin through the trees in that direction.

He applied the brakes, stopping the Mustang.

It would not do to drive right up to the build-ing. Their man and his lady would be watching for that, and even if they were dumb enough not to be - Jayme rather doubted that - driving up would make noise and draw their attention.

Jayme looked around for a moment, then turned the Mustang to the right and, moving very slowly, slipped it off to the side of the trail, where the trees offered a few feet of clearance. Not that he expected anyone else to drive up here. But he did not like the notion of blocking the only road out of there, just in case.

Shutting off the car's engine, Jayme pulled his Sig out and took a deep breath. Then he nodded to Rolf and opened the car door.

JAYME CREPT up to the cabin's back door while Rolf approached a window a few feet to the right. It was quiet. He could almost believe there was no one inside, except for the Mazda parked out front and the smoke wisping out of the chimney.

They were in there, all right.

He reached the door and slowly tried the knob. It turned freely in his hand; unlocked.

A glance over at Rolf, long enough to see the other man's nod, told him all he needed to know. The coast was clear, at least in the rear of the house.

Slowly, carefully, he pulled the door open. It moved smoothly on its hinges, making barely a sound. That was a relief; Jayme had been screwed by squeaking hinges a couple times. But not this time. It was all starting to come together.

He smiled thinly and stepped inside, Rolf close behind.

The back room was a kitchen. Small, with appliances that dated from the 60s probably, it nevertheless was a pleasant place. The scent of baked bread lingered in the air, making Jayme's mouth water. The lady of the house was handy with the oven, it seemed. His kind of girl.

Jayme moved carefully, on the balls of his feet to minimize his noise, to the doorway leading deeper into the house. Sig held up beside his face, he stopped at the edge of the doorway and eased his head forward so he could peek around.

The next room was a combination dining room and living room - some folks call those great rooms, said the part of his mind that he usually turned off in these circumstances. The furniture was dated, just like the kitchen, but everything was tidy and arranged just so. Off to the left, near the cabin's front door, a set of stairs led to the upper level, probably where the bedrooms were located.

A woman, the woman from the car, stood with her back to Jayme, looking out the front window.

She was naked.

Jayme did a double-take.

She was still naked. And Lord, did she have a great ass.

Jayme swallowed and flexed his fingers around the grip of his Sig. Trying not to think about the view in front of him, he glanced back over his shoulder toward Rolf and pointed the first two fingers of his left hand toward his eyes, then held up his index finger. I see one person.

Rolf nodded. Let's do it.

Jayme took a deep breath then looked back around the corner again.

She was still there. Still naked. But she was now facing the kitchen, and for a moment, he enjoyed the full frontal view. Her ass had nothing on her front. Glory be!

Their eyes met, and hers widened in surprised shock. No time to stop and admire the view.

Jayme lowered his Sig and stepped fully into

the room, painfully aware of the fact that he was about the burst his pants from the hard-on he was growing. He did his best to ignore it, though, as he sighted the weapon in on her, center of mass.

"Don't move," he ordered in his coldest, most business-like tone.

Rolf bolted around the corner a second later, his Beretta held at the ready. He stopped abruptly upon seeing the woman.

"Holy shit," he said breathlessly.

For a moment, they stood there, the two of them with their weapons trained on the woman. She frozen in mid-movement, her eyes flickering between their faces, then lowering as she no doubt noticed the effect she was having on them.

Jayme cursed nature right then. How could you make a woman believe you were going to blow her away when your body told her you really wanted *her* to blow *you*?

Her lips curled upward slightly. She knew her advantage, despite their having the drop on her.

Shit.

A single gunshot, from off to the left, broke the spell.

* * *

THE BULLET WHIZZED past Jayme's head and he felt his hair ruffle from the wake it left in the air.

That was *way* too close.

Pivoting on his heel, Jayme saw his man.

He stood halfway down the staircase from the second level, dressed only in his boxer shorts. He was ready for his lady, but that tent was quickly lowering. In his hands was a fair-sized revolver, probably a .357, but from the awkward way he was recovering from the gun's recoil, he did not shoot very often, at least not with a weapon of that caliber.

He had a wild look in his eyes, as though he was scared out of his wits.

Jayme did not pause to consider why the guy had carried a gun down from upstairs if he was planning to bang his girlfriend, or whatever she was. He just dropped to one knee, sighted in, and fired before the guy could recover enough from the revolver's recoil to fire again.

Jayme's round struck the man in the shoulder. He pinwheeled around into the wall, then lost his balance and tumbled down the staircase to the landing before the front door.

From behind him, Rolf shouted an oath that became a cry of pain.

Jayme spun back around and saw the woman, still naked but clutching a knife like a trained fighter, pull back from Rolf as he stumbled forward. Her blade dripped red spots onto the floor, and Jayme could see a corresponding cut on his partner's thigh.

Rolf fell to his knee, but managed to stabilize himself before hitting the ground completely.

The woman noticed Jayme turning back toward her and crouched, then spun around behind Rolf. It was going to be hard to shoot her without hitting him, but Jayme brought his Sig to bear, looking for his shot.

Rolf ruined it. He tried to turn his weapon on the woman as well, but she continued to move.

She was fast, much faster than Jayme would have thought. One moment she was behind Rolf as he turned toward her, the next, she was at his side, his left arm - he was a lefty - in a lock that made him arch his back and grimace in pain...and point his gun directly at Jayme.

The woman smiled and gave a little jerk of her shoulders, and Rolf cried out again. Jayme could only watch in shock as his partner's finger clenched on the trigger in reaction.

The round hit Jayme dead center in the gut, crumpling him over and sending him to the ground before he realized what had happened.

Then the pain hit, and it was all he could do to hold back a scream.

He tried to raise his gun before she finished him, but there was no time.

The woman wrenched Rolf's arm again, and his hand went limp, dropping his Beretta into her hand. Then she kicked his good leg out from under him and turned fully toward Jayme, taking careful aim at him.

"Lose the gun," she ordered, her voice cool and calm.

Jayme was impressed to see that she had not broken a sweat, and was not even breathing heavily. But then, that she was in great shape was obvious just from looking at her. She was a sight to see, for certain. But just then, Jayme was not surprised to realize he was not that interested.

Slowly, he raised his gun hand - he feared what would happen with his belly if he took his other hand from the wound - and tossed the Sig off to the side.

Then he waited for the kill shot.

She did not fire. Instead, her eyes flickered past Jayme toward the man at the bottom of the stairs.

"You ok, baby?"

A low groan was his initial reply, but then he managed, "It hurts like a bitch!" It sounded like he was clenching his teeth.

"Get up. We have to go."

"Babe, I..."

"*Now!*"

Jayme heard the man struggling to his feet, but never took his eyes off the woman.

She licked her lips and stepped away from him and Rolf, toward the couch where, Jayme could see now, her clothing lay haphazardly. Taking one hand off the gun, she scooped up the garments and pressed them against her side to hold them tight. Her aim remained steady the whole time.

"Get the bag and let's get out of here."

The man whimpered, but Jayme heard him slowly maneuver upstairs. A few moments later, he came back down. From the sound of it, he almost fell down the stairs twice.

The woman circled around toward the door. Jayme followed her with her eyes. Against his better judgment, hope blossomed within him. If she was going to finish them off, she would have done it by now. Wouldn't she?

At the door, she looked away from Jayme long enough to give her man a quick once-over. Then she jerked her head toward the door. While the man stepped outside, she returned her gaze to Jayme and Rolf.

"Don't follow us. You won't get off this easy next time." She spoke with such a confident assurance that, even had he not witnessed her prowess first hand a moment before, Jayme would have believed her.

Then she stepped through the door and out of sight.

Two gunshots rang out from the front of the house.

A moment later, Jayme saw Ismerelda through the open door.

ISMERELDA STOPPED a few feet away from Jayme and Rolf. She wore a disapproving expression as she looked down at them.

"Gentlemen," she said. "That did not go as well as I would have hoped."

Jayme managed a half-shrug. Or at least he tried to, but moving even that much sent a new wave of pain through his belly.

Rolf did the talking this time. "How the hell did *you* get here?"

"My man planted a GPS tracker on your car while we spoke earlier." She looked around the room and pursed her lips. "Sloppy. Very sloppy."

Rolf glowered at her. "You could have warned us he was meeting a ninja."

Ismerelda quirked an eyebrow upward at his words. "You could have done a better job researching your target before you went in with guns blazing." She shook her head, then gestured with her left hand.

The guard on that side stepped forward and reached inside his suit coat. Jayme cringed, but when the man's hand came back out, it held an envelope, not a gun.

Ismerelda took the proffered envelope and flicked it open. After a quick check of its contents, she nodded quickly, then tossed it onto the floor.

"Your money," she said, by way of explanation. "We will not meet again."

Then she turned away from them. The guards exited the room and she made to follow. But she paused before stepping through the door, looking back at Jayme with icy eyes.

"I took the liberty of calling for assistance. Ambulances are on the way, if you wish to wait for them." She smiled then, a smile that was just as cold as her eyes. "I expect the Police will be along as well. Good luck!"

And then she was gone.

"Ah fuck," Rolf said. He forced himself to his feet, grimacing. "We gotta get out of here."

Rolf limped over to the envelope and picked it up, grunting with every movement. Stuffing the money in his pocket, he turned to Jayme and offered his right hand.

Somehow they managed to get Jayme up on his feet. Then they set off toward the door, and the Mustang. Jayme had to lean on Rolf's shoulder for support. It was excruciating, but he really did not want to be there when the cops showed up.

"You got the car keys?"

Jayme nodded and fumbled into his pocket for them.

They made it as far as the door. Then Jayme's legs buckled, and Rolf could not stop him from falling again.

He hit the floor and cried out as renewed pain flared out of the wound. Vaguely, he heard the keys strike the floor a couple feet away, but his entire world was pain for a long minute and he paid it no mind.

When he managed to resolve anything besides the pain of his wound, Rolf was standing over him, the car keys clutched in his right hand. From the bulge under his arm, his Beretta was back in its shoulder holster; he must have retrieved it from the woman's corpse outside.

Rolf met Jayme's gaze in silence for a long moment. In addition to the pain in his belly, Jayme began to get a cold feeling in the pit of his stomach from the look on the other man's face.

"This isn't going to work, partner," Rolf said.

"No. Rolf, we can…"

"No time. Hear that?"

Sure enough, now that Rolf mentioned it, Jayme *could* hear it. Faint, but getting slowly louder.

Sirens.

"Been good working with you, brother."

And then Rolf turned and limped down the front porch and toward the Mustang, back where they left it on the trail leading to the house.

As he heard the car start and saw the rising dust as Rolf sped away, Jayme collapsed back onto the floor, his breath coming in quick pants. He listened to the sirens growing louder and found, however much he wanted to, that he could not curse Rolf for leaving him to the Cops.

After all, it was just business.

Message From The Author

Thank you for reading my book. I hope you enjoyed reading it as much as I enjoyed writing it.

Every review helps an author out, so whether you loved this book, hated it, or something in between, please take a minute to tell other readers what you thought. All of the online retailers make it very easy to do, and I would really appreciate it.

Feel free to come say hi at my website or on Facebook. I always enjoy hearing from readers, especially since you all are, collectively, my boss.

I also have a weekly podcast, Story Time With Michael Kingswood, where I read stories and talk through some of the latest goings on in my world. I'd love to see you there.

Thanks again. My best to you and yours.

Warm Regards,
Michael Kingswood

Mailing List

If you enjoyed this book and would like word on new releases and special deals from Michael Kingswood, sign up for his newsletter on his website. Guaranteed to be spam-free, you can opt out at any time. And you can rest assured he will not share your information with anyone, for any reason.

https://michaelkingswood.com/newsletter-signup/

Supporting Patronage

Michael would like to invite you to become a supporting member of his website. Similar in concept to Patreon, a few dollars a month will give you access to exclusive content, and help him to focus more of his time to writing fun and exciting stories for your enjoyment.

Sign up at his website:

https://www.michaelkingswood.com/
membership/supporting-patronage/

About The Author

Michael Kingswood is 20-year veteran of the US Navy submarine force and a lifelong fan of science fiction and fantasy literature. His work has appeared in numerous collections and anthologies, to include the Fiction River Anthology series from WMG publishing. He holds a bachelors degree in Mechanical Engineering as well as a Master of Engineering Management and a Master of Business Administration. He has four children and currently resides in San Diego.

Find Michael Kingswood online at:

www.michaelkingswood.com

www.facebook.com/michael.kingswood

steemit.com/@michaelkingswood

The Champion
Veritas Morte

Story Collections

Tales Of Adventure #1

Tales Of Adventure #2

Short Story 10-Pack

A Jar Of Mixed Treats

Short Fiction

Michael has also published a number of shorter works,
links to which can be found on his website.

 Created with Vellum

www.ingramcontent.com/pod-product-compliance
Lightning Source LLC
Chambersburg PA
CBHW032053180726
48284CB00004B/1325